P9-CRZ-783

HISTORICAL TALES

The Plot on the Pyramid

by Terry Deary

illustrated by Helen Flook

PICTURE WINDOW BOOKS
Minneapolis, Minnesota

Editor: Julie Gassman
Story Consultant: Terry Flaherty
Page Production: Tracy Davies
Creative Director: Keith Griffin
Editorial Director: Carol Jones
Managing Editor: Catherine Neitge

First American edition published in 2006 by
Picture Window Books
5115 Excelsior Boulevard
Suite 232
Minneapolis, MN 55416
1-877-845-8392
www.picturewindowbooks.com

First published in Great Britain by
A & C Black Publishers Limited
37 Soho Square, London W1D 3QZ

Library of Congress Cataloging-in-Publication Data
Deary, Terry.
The plot on the pyramid / by Terry Deary; illustrated by Helen Flook.
p. cm. — (Historical tales) (Read it! chapter books)
Summary: A clever trick saves the workers who are building the Great Pyramid from being punished, and their working conditions are improved as well.
Includes bibliographical references.
ISBN 1-4048-1273-3 (hardcover)
[1. Pyramids—Egypt—Fiction. 2. Egypt—Civilization–To 332 B.C. —Fiction.] I. Flook, Helen, ill. II. Title. III. Series: Deary, Terry. Historical tales. IV. Series: Read it! chapter books.
PZ7.D3517Plo 2005
[Fic]—dc22 2005007196

Printed in the United States of America.

Table of Contents

Akhet (AHK-et)
Antef (AHNT-ef)
Amenemhat (AH-men-EM-hat)
Nephoris (NEF-or-is)
Oneney (on-EN-ay-ee)
Pere (peh-RAY)
Yenini (YEH-nee-nee)

Chapter 1

River and Rat

Nephoris sat by the edge of the mud-brown river and threw a stone into it. She was a tall girl and made her little brother Pere look tiny.

A light wind kept her cool, and the rustling reeds seemed the only sound in the world. "Perfect," she said.

Of course, that was before her mother called her home.

"River," Pere said. He picked up a stone and tried to copy Nephoris's throwing. But he forgot to let go of the stone and threw himself into the dirty water.

Nephoris shook her head, paddled into the cool water, and pulled him out.

"It's Akhet," she told him.

The little boy's round face crinkled into a frown. "No Akhet. River."

She sat beside him and watched the graceful ibis birds land and stalk through the shallows, looking for food.

"I mean it's the time of the year—Akhet. It is the time when the river rises. It floods our fields and makes the corn grow. Akhet brings us food."

"Food," Pere repeated. Pere liked food.

Nephoris smiled. There weren't many restful days like this when she could sit in the sun and play with Pere.

She had
to weed
the fields,

fetch water,

grind corn, or
bake bread.

She'd worked ever since she was as young as Pere, but not at Akhet.

"When Akhet comes, we can't work in the fields. So we get days like today ... peaceful days," she sighed.

Of course, that was before her mother called her home. In the years to come, Nephoris would never think of Akhet as the peaceful time again.

Pere took a fistful of mud and made it into a little pile. "Pyramid," he said.

Nephoris nodded. "Yes, Daddy is working on the pyramid for the king. Most of the men of Lisht are helping to build it because they can't work in the fields during Akhet. Poor Dad. We have idle days, and he works harder than ever."

Pere made his chubby hand into a fist and smashed it down on top of his mud pile. "Pyramid!" he giggled.

"Poor pyramid," Nephoris said. "King Amenemhat is our god, you know. He makes the river flood the fields and makes the corn grow. That's why we are building Amenemhat a huge pyramid. Build Amenemhat another pyramid," she said.

As Pere piled up the mud, a ripple from the river washed it away. The river was rising fast now. Amenemhat was doing his magic.

Pere frowned at the river and his ruined pyramid. "Naughty!" he said. He slapped the water. It splashed up and soaked his angry face. Nephoris laughed. Life was good.

Then her mother called her home.

Her shrill voice carried over the quiet fields. "Nephoris!"

"Mama!" Pere said, struggling to his feet. He had sharp ears and heard her first. Nephoris quickly washed his muddy legs and hands, scooped him up, and ran along the dusty path toward their small mud house.

At the Pyramid of Lisht, their father Yenini was getting more and more angry.

Chapter 2

The Boat Gang

Yenini's face was red. Red with the heat of the midday sun. Red with the strain of pulling a pyramid block almost to the top of Amenemhat's pyramid. But most of all, it was red with rage for the fat little bully, Antef.

Thirty men from Lisht made up a team of workers. They called themselves the Boat Gang. They were proud of being the best of the hundred gangs that worked on the pyramid.

The Pharaoh had put Antef—with his perfumed wig, fake beard, pot belly, and wicked tongue—in charge.

The Boat Gang were free men. They worked for the love of King Amenemhat. Antef treated them like the prisoners of war who were beaten and forced to work.

The day had started badly. Their massive stone, big as a house, had slipped off the barge that carried it over the river Nile. They had to fasten ropes around it and drag it through the mud and onto the shore.

Yenini was a little worried that they would not get it up the pyramid before sunset. He didn't like the Boat Gang to fail. They never had before.

They heaved the stone onto a wooden sled, and the sled cracked. It was an old sled. Antef should have got them a better one.

Yenini was a bit upset by that.

The cracked sled was even harder to pull. It took them most of the morning to get it to the foot of the pyramid. Yenini was getting hungry. When the sun passed the peak of the pyramid, they could take a rest and eat in the shadowed side of the tomb.

But the sled stuck on the ramp that led to the top.

Yenini was annoyed.

"Come on, Boat Gang," he cried. "Put your backs into it. There's a neat little hole at the top just waiting for this stone. There's an even bigger hole in my stomach waiting for my dinner!"

The men laughed and tried harder. They sweated and strained, and the huge stone moved upward.

That was when Antef really upset them. He walked behind them and watched.

"Laughing are you? Laughing. You are the biggest bunch of brainless beetles on this pyramid. All you can do is laugh. You can't move one little stone, and you think it's funny?" he jeered. Antef cracked his leather whip, snapping it in the air close to Yenini's nose.

"Hang on, Antef," Yenini said. "It's your fault that we have this cracked, old sled. It's your job to see we get the best." He was getting angry.

The stone reached the edge of the hole, and the Boat Gang began to turn it so it would slide down neatly into the space.

Antef shook his whip in Yenini's face. "I am the servant of Amenemhat. It is the king who tells me what my job is. It's not your job to tell me my job. It's my job to tell you your job," he lectured. "That's my job, and I'm doing my job. You do your job, or my job will be to send you to the king to be punished."

"Don't threaten me!" Yenini roared. He let go of the rope and stepped toward Antef. The little man jumped back in fear. His foot slipped on the edge of the hole, and he slipped down into it.

The hole was just too deep for him to climb out. "Throw me a rope, you desert snakes, you river rats, you savage scorpions, you ... you ... slimy ox dung!"

Yenini was red with rage. “It is time for lunch.”

“You take lunch when I say you can take lunch! The king is coming this afternoon. He wants to see this stone in place. You will *not* stop for lunch. I forbid it,” Antef wailed. “Get me out of here!”

The Boat Gang looked at each other. They dropped the ropes and walked back down the pyramid for a rest.

Meanwhile...

Back in the village, Nephoris was carrying Pere home.

Chapter 3

The Slipping Stone

Yenini's family lived in a village on the edge of Lisht. That morning, the people were working in the shade of the houses, but one man worked in the full glare of the sun.

Using precious cedar wood, the artist Oneney was building a large statue.

"Big man," Pere said.

"Statue," Nephoris explained. "It's a statue of King Amenemhat. When he dies, the statue will go inside the pyramid with the king's mummy."

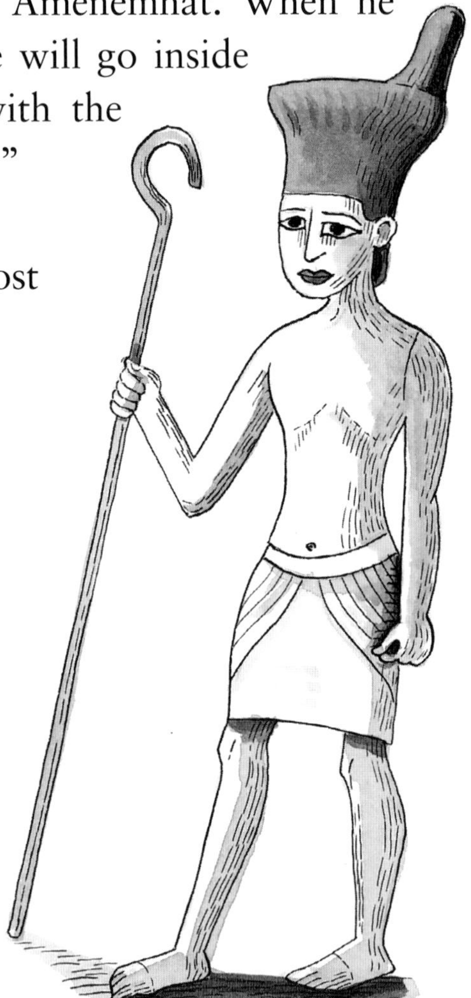

The king's statue was almost finished. It was dressed in a white kilt and carried a shepherd's crook. The life-sized model had one leg in front of the other, as if it was striding forward.

Beside it stood a finished model of a small, round man in a wig, fake beard, and purple robes. It was no taller than Nephoris.

"That's a model of Antef, the work-driver," Nephoris told her brother. "That will go in the pyramid, too, so the dead king has company. Dad doesn't like Antef."

"Naughty man," Pere said. He slapped the model.

Oneney was painting the crown on Amenemhat's head bright red. A bowl was full of red paint.

“Blood,” Pere said as Nephoris carried him past the artist.

Oneney shook his head. “No, young Pere. Beetles. I crush beetles to make the red color.”

Nephoris shuddered, but Pere just looked puzzled.

“Your mother is looking for you,” Oneney told her.

“I heard her calling. What does she want?” Nephoris asked.

Oneney shrugged.

Nephoris's mother stood at the door of their house. She was holding a small package wrapped in cloth.

"What's wrong?" Nephoris asked.

Her mother held out the parcel. "Last night, the cat caught a rat and left it in the middle of the floor—a nice present for us. I didn't want Pere picking it up and chewing at it. You know what he's like."

"Rat," Pere said, licking his lips.

"This morning, your father set off for work at the pyramid. I packed him some bread and onion like I always do," her mother went on.

"Yes," Nephoris said.

"Well, when I went to throw the rat away, I opened the parcel and found the bread and onion!" she moaned.

"So," Nephoris grinned, "when Dad opens his lunch parcel he'll find ..."

"Rat!" Pere said.

"Exactly! He'll be furious! He's in a bad mood all the time these days. That Antef bullies the workers all day long, from sunrise to sunset. Your dad comes home and he's full of fury. If he goes without food all day, he will be as horrible as ... as ... "

"Rat," Pere said.

"Exactly," Mother agreed. "A big, bad-tempered rat." She looked up at the clear sky. The sun was not far from its highest point. "They'll be stopping soon for a break," she said. "You have to get this food to him before they stop!"

"Don't worry, Mom," Nephoris said. "I can run faster than anyone in this village. Give me the food."

She put her brother on the ground, took the parcel, and sped toward the site of the pyramid.

Nephoris raced the sun. Her black hair flowed behind her, and her long legs raised clouds of dust. "I'm winning, Sun, I'm winning," she cried.

At last, she reached the wall around the site. She ran up to the first gang leader she could find. "Boat Gang," she panted. "Where will I find the Boat Gang?"

The man pointed toward the top of the huge pyramid. "Working up there today—better them than me!" he grunted.

Nephoris groaned. The sun raced on, and this time it was winning.

As Nephoris reached the foot of the pyramid, she saw her father and the Boat Gang stomping down with heavy feet and grim faces. "Just in time," she muttered. "He looks in a rotten temper. If he'd opened his lunch pack and found a rat, he might have eaten it in anger!"

Yenini glared at Nephoris. "What are you doing here? It's a dangerous place for a child. What is your mother thinking of? Wait until I get home."

"But I came to bring ..." Nephoris began.

Then there was a rumble, and the men of the Boat Gang turned and looked up at the pyramid.

At the top of the pyramid ...

Chapter 4

Peril at the Pyramid

The Boat Gang had left their stone at the edge of the hole. The old wooden sled grew hotter and drier in the midday sun. It creaked a little, then it cracked.

The stone sank into the sled and turned it to splinters and dust. Finally the stone began to slip. It slipped steadily into the hole that was waiting for it. The stone landed with a "whumph."

It was a perfect fit. It would stay there until long after the Boat Gang finished their work, long after Amenemhat was buried inside, and long after the grave robbers stole his wealth. It would stay there until the end of time.

Yenini raced up the steep ramp. He was the fastest of the Lisht men—smooth and swift like his daughter. Nephoris ran behind him. She caught him up at the top of the pyramid. She could see clear across Lisht, over her village, and over the mud-brown flowing Nile.

Her father's redness shrank to a spot on each cheek. The rest of his face and body was pale and sweating. "What's wrong?" Nephoris asked. "It fell where it was supposed to. It saved you the work!"

"We'll never get it out," her father whispered. The men of the Boat Gang panted and wheezed up to his side.

"Why would you want to get it out?" Nephoris asked, puzzled.

Yenini looked at her with haunted eyes. "Because little Antef is underneath that stone," he groaned. "Crushed."

"Like Oneney's beetles," Nephoris said.

"We've killed the king's man. Now the king will kill us," one of the workers moaned.

"It was an accident," Nephoris said.

"We all hated him," Yenini sighed. "No one will believe it was an accident."

"The king is coming this afternoon," a man said. "How do you think he will kill us?"

"Club us to death," someone suggested.

"Too quick and painless. Probably tie us to stakes in the desert and leave us to rot. Let the jackals eat us," another man argued.

They all began to wail and sob. "Throw us into a pit of poisoned snakes!" came one loud cry.

Suddenly, a voice called out louder than all the rest. "Stop it! Stop this pitiful noise!" Nephoris cried.

They stopped. They looked at the girl. "We're going to die-ie-ie!" an old man whimpered.

"No, you are not!" Nephoris said. "Get back to work. There is another stone waiting on the barge by the river. Get it on a sled. Drag it up the pyramid. That's what you must be doing when the king arrives. Showing how hard you work for him—how much you worship him."

She waved a hand at the scene below. "Look! The Nile is flooding. Amenemhat has brought you life for another year. Let him see how much you love him. Get building!"

Yenini frowned. "He will want to see Antef driving us."

"And he will see Antef driving you," Nephoris promised.

"We can't pull him out from under the stone," a man argued.

"And if we did he'd be a bit … flat," Yenini argued.

"Just *do* it!" Nephoris said. "I'll have Antef with you by the time you have the next stone at the foot of the pyramid."

The men looked bewildered but wandered back down the pyramid to obey her. Nephoris raced past them like an antelope and set off across the plain to Lisht.

King Amenemhat's boat drifted down the cool waters of the Nile and headed for Lisht.

Chapter 5

The Dead Driver

King Amenemhat was carried in a shaded chair. That's the only way for a god to travel. When he reached the pyramid, he opened the curtain and looked out. His face was as calm as the carved lions in the temple, but inside he was excited.

He watched the Boat Gang heaving on the ropes and singing a hymn. A hymn about their glorious King Amenemhat. His Majesty was pleased.

Walking alongside the Boat Gang was a little man with a perfumed wig and beard. Between the lines of the hymn, the king could hear the little man shouting. It was not very pleasant.

"You are the biggest bunch of brainless beetles on this pyramid. All you can do is sing. You can't move one little stone, and you think it's something to sing about?" he shouted in his voice that was thin as a Nile reed.

He raised the whip and tried to crack it. The end of the whip lashed back and caught him on the end of his nose.

"Don't laugh, you rabble of rats! Ouch! Ouch! Ouch! If one man laughs, I will have him taken to the top of the pyramid and thrown off! Now h-e-a-v-e!"

King Amenemhat said to a servant, "Send Antef to me."

The servant hurried off and brought the little work-driver back. Antef held a hand to his injured nose and kept his eyes on the sizzling sand. All King Amenemhat could see was the dark wig and fake beard.

"Is the work going well, Antef?" the king asked.

"Very, very well. We shall be finished by harvest time. That Boat Gang from Lisht is wonderful."

"You shout at them a lot!"

"Ah, but only because we all love you so much, we want to do better than our best for you," Antef said humbly.

"Better than your best ... is that the best you can do?"

"It's better," Antef muttered. "May I get back to work now, your majesty? They will be dropping that stone in place soon, and I need to be there. We don't want any more accidents."

"Any more?" the king said. "Have there been any others?"

"No, your majesty," Antef said, a little confused. "Just the odd crushed beetle. Nothing to worry about."

"Beetles?"

"Crushed."

The king leaned forward and peered at the work-driver. "Are you all right, Antef?" Antef pulled out a large rag and covered his face with it.

"Sorry, Majesty," he sniffled. "It was my favorite beetle."

The king blew out his cheeks. "Antef. I think the sun has boiled your brain. Go home and rest until you feel better. Make one of the Boat Gang the new work-driver."

"Yenini is very good, your majesty."

"Very well, Yenini is the new work-driver," he said and leaned back. "Servants! Take me back to the palace."

The covered chair was carried away.

If the king had looked back, he'd have seen Antef tear off his itchy wig and scratchy beard, then run up the pyramid to where Yenini was waiting.

Antef ran with the stride of a gazelle, and the padding fell out of his robes. He no longer looked like a fat little work-driver. He looked more like a girl named Nephoris hugging her father Yenini.

Maybe ... it was.

Chapter 6

A Rat in the Grass

Nephoris walked home, arm-in-arm with her father, over the fields. She was carrying a purple robe, a perfumed wig, and a fake beard. When they reached their village, she handed them back to the artist Oneney, and soon the fat statue of Antef was as good as new.

"I'm starving," Yenini said. "With all that bother at the pyramid, I didn't even have time to eat my lunch."

"Your dinner is ready now," his wife said.

"No, it's a pity to waste good food," the man said. He pulled out his lunch packet and unwrapped it.

"Oh, Dad ..." Nephoris began.

It was too late. Yenini was staring at a fat, dead rat. He gave a roar that could be heard at the top of the pyramid. He threw the rat through the open doorway into the long grass. His curses would have frightened the demons of the underworld.

He was roaring so loudly that he didn't hear the little cry of fear coming from the grass where the rat had landed.

But little Pere's sharp ears heard it. He pulled himself onto his stumpy legs and wandered out of the house. "Rats," he muttered.

The stars were burning in the purple sky, and a thin moon glittered on the inky Nile. Pere carefully pulled the grass apart and saw the man lying there—a short, fat, bald man. The dead rat was resting on his bald head where it had landed. He was quivering and too terrified to move it.

"Rats," Pere said.

"Oh, little boy, hush. Don't give me away. Spare me, and I'll see the king gives you a purse of gold. But don't tell the men of Lisht I am here."

"Little man," Pere said.

"They tried to kill me, you know. Left me in a hole and went to eat their lunch. I was lucky. I caught one of the ropes on the sled and pulled myself up. But I was a bit too heavy. I pulled the stone down. It fell just after I scrambled out. Oh, but I ran down the other side of the pyramid. They didn't see me. I bet they think they killed me!"

"Naughty man," Pere said. He picked up the dead rat and slapped Antef across the head with it. It fell to the ground.

"I've taken off my wig and beard so no one will know me," Antef babbled. "I've been hiding here all afternoon with the earwigs and spiders. When the moon sets I'll go down to the port and take the next boat out of Lisht. I'll never come back. Never. They hate me."

Pere giggled.

"But I am so hungry," Antef groaned. "Can you give me something to eat, little boy? Please, please get me food. Do you understand? Food? FOOD ..."

Pere looked hard at the man with a face-crumpling frown. Then he smiled his one-toothed smile. He reached to the ground and said, "Food!"

He picked up the rat and stuffed it into Antef's mouth.

Afterword

The Egyptians worked hard to build the massive stone pyramids for their kings. They worked in groups and had names like the Boat Gang.

These men were paid in food, so building a pyramid wouldn't make them rich. But they were proud to do this service for the king, who was their god. They believed their king-god made the river Nile flood. This flood each year made sure their crops grew.

While the fields were flooded, they were free to work on the pyramids. It seems some of the king's officers treated the workers badly. They treated them like slaves, and the proud peasants didn't like that. In 1170 b.c. the workers organized what was the first ever strike.

The workers marched together into the temple, refusing to work. They complained about a lack of food, drink, clothing, and medicine. A scribe wrote down their complaints. Their message finally reached the king, who arranged for the men to be paid with corn. Strikes of this kind happened again during the reign of Ramses III and later pharaohs.

There were many accidents on these dangerous building sites. Some might have been deliberate. "Oooops! Sorry I dropped that 20 ton block on your head, boss!"

Look for all the

by best-selling author Terry Deary

The Actor, the Rebel, and the Wrinkled Queen

The Maid, the Witch, and the Cruel Queen

The Prince, the Cook, and the Cunning King

The Thief, the Fool, and the Big Fat King

The Gold in the Grave

The Magic and the Mummy

The Phantom and the Fisherman

The Plot on the Pyramid

www

vernon community Amish- $1.500
1205 rabure rd
Hestand, KY 42151

m - 7:30 a.m - 3:00 P.M
T - 7:30 a.m - 3:00 P.M
sa- w - Th Close
F 7:30 a.m. - 3:00 P.M
S 7:30 am 11:30 P.M
b